Jonathan Cleaned Up—
Then He Heard a Sound

or *Blackberry Subway Jam*

STORY by ROBERT MUNSCH

ART by MICHAEL MARTCHENKO

annick press
toronto • berkeley

We acknowledge the support of the Canada Council for the Arts and the Ontario Arts Council, and the participation of the Government of Canada/la participation du gouvernement du Canada for our publishing activities.

Library and Archives Canada Cataloguing in Publication

Munsch, Robert N., 1945-, author
    Jonathan cleaned up, then he heard a sound / Robert Munsch ; [illustrations by] Michael Martchenko.

(Classic Munsch)
Previously published: Toronto : Annick Press, ©1981.
ISBN 978-1-77321-089-6 (hardcover).--ISBN 978-1-77321-088-9 (softcover)

    I. Martchenko, Michael, illustrator II. Title.

PS8576.U575J65 2018   jC813'.54   C2018-901421-0

Published in the U.S.A. by Annick Press (U.S.) Ltd.
Distributed in Canada by University of Toronto Press.
Distributed in the U.S.A. by Publishers Group West.

Printed in China

www.annickpress.com
www.robertmunsch.com

Also available in e-book format. Please visit www.annickpress.com/ebooks.html for more details.

To Andrew

Jonathan's mother went to get a can of noodles. She said, "Jonathan, please don't make a mess!"

When she was gone, Jonathan stood in the middle of the apartment and looked at the nice clean rug and the nice clean walls and the very, very clean sofa and said, "Well, there is certainly no mess here."

Then he heard a sound. It was coming from behind the wall. He put his ear up against the wall and listened very carefully.

The noise sounded like a train. Just then, the wall slid open and a subway train pulled up and stopped. Someone yelled, "**LAST STOP! EVERYBODY OUT!**"

Then little people, big people, fat people and thin people, and all kinds of people, came out of Jonathan's wall, ran around his apartment, and went out the front door.

Jonathan stood in the middle of the living room and looked around. There was writing on the wall, gum on the rug and a man sleeping on the sofa, and all the food was gone from the refrigerator.

"Well," said Jonathan, "this is certainly a mess!" Jonathan tried to drag the man out the door, but he met his mother coming in.

She saw the writing on the wall, the gum on the rug, and the empty refrigerator. She yelled, "Jonathan, what a mess!"

Jonathan said, "The wall opened up and there was a subway train. Thousands of people came running through."

But his mother said, "Oh, Jon, don't be silly. Clean it up."

She went out to get another can of noodles, and Jonathan cleaned up. When he was all done, he heard a sound. It was coming from behind the wall. He put his ear up against the wall and listened very carefully.

The noise sounded like a train. Just then, the wall slid open and there was a subway train. Someone yelled, "**LAST STOP! EVERYBODY OUT!**"

And all kinds of people came out of Jonathan's wall, ran around his apartment, and went out the front door.

This time there were ice cream cones and chewing gum on the rug, writing and footprints on the wall, two men sleeping on the sofa, and a policeman watching TV. Besides that, the refrigerator was gone.

Jonathan got angry and yelled, "Everybody out."

Just then his mother came in. She saw ice cream cones and chewing gum on the rug, writing and footprints on the wall, two men sleeping on the sofa, a policeman watching TV, and a big empty space where the refrigerator had been. "Jonathan," she said, "what have you done?"

Then she heard a noise. It was coming from behind the wall. She put her ear right against the wall and listened very carefully. The noise sounded like a train. Just then the wall slid open and a subway train pulled up. Someone yelled, **"LAST STOP! EVERYBODY OUT!"**

And all kinds of people ran out of Jonathan's wall, ran around his apartment, and went out the front door.

There were ice cream cones, chewing gum and pretzel bags on the rug, writing and footprints and handprints on the wall, and five men sleeping on the sofa. Besides that, a policeman and a conductor were watching TV, and the fridge and stove were gone.

Jonathan went to the conductor and said, "This is not a subway station, this is my house!"

The conductor said, "If the subway stops here, then it's a subway station! You shouldn't build your house in a subway station. If you don't like it, go see City Hall."

So Jonathan went to City Hall.

When he got there, the lady at the front desk told him to see the subway boss, and the subway boss told Jonathan to go see the Mayor.

So he went and saw the Mayor. The Mayor said, "If the subway stops there, then it's a subway station! You shouldn't build your house in a subway station. Our computer says it's a subway station, and our computer is never wrong." Then he ran out for lunch.

In fact, everyone ran out for lunch, and Jonathan was all by himself at City Hall. Jonathan started to leave, but on his way out he heard a sound.

Someone was crying, "Oooooooh, I'm hungry."

Jonathan listened very carefully. He walked up and down the hall and found the room it was coming from. He went in, and there was a big, enormous, shining computer machine. The computer was going "wing, wing, kler-klung, clickety clang," and its lights were going off and on. The voice was coming from behind it.

Jonathan squeezed in back of the machine and saw a little old man at a very messy desk. The man looked at Jonathan and said, "Do you have any blackberry jam?"

"No," said Jonathan, "but I could get you some. Who are you?"

"I'm the computer," said the man.

Now, Jonathan was no dummy. He said, "Computers are machines, and you are not a machine. They go 'wing, wing, kler-klung, clickety clang.'"

The man pointed at the big computer and said, "Well, that goes 'wing, wing, kler-klung, clickety clang,' but the darn thing never did work. I do everything for the whole city."

"Oh," said Jonathan. "I will get you some blackberry jam if you'll do me a favor. A subway station is in my house at 980 Young Street. Please change it."

"Certainly," said the old man. "I remember doing that. I didn't know where to put it."

Jonathan ran out and passed all the offices with nobody there. He ran down the stairs and all the way to a jam store. He got four cases of jam. It took him three hours to carry it all the way back to City Hall. There was still nobody there. He carried the jam back behind the computer and put it on the floor.

"Now," said the old man, "where am I going to put this subway station?"

"I know," said Jonathan, and he whispered in the old man's ear. Then he left. But the old man yelled after him, "Don't tell anyone the computer is broken. The Mayor would be very upset. He paid ten million dollars for it."

When Jonathan got home, his mother was still standing on the rug, because she was stuck to the gum.

Jonathan started washing the writing off the wall. He said, "There will be no more subways here."

And he was right.

Even More Classic Munsch:

Classic Munsch ABC
The Dark
Mud Puddle
The Paper Bag Princess
The Boy in the Drawer
Millicent and the Wind
Mortimer
Murmel, Murmel, Murmel
The Fire Station
Angela's Airplane
David's Father
Thomas' Snowsuit
50 Below Zero
I Have to Go!
Moira's Birthday
A Promise is a Promise
Pigs
Something Good
Show and Tell
Purple, Green and Yellow
Wait and See
Where is Gah-Ning?
From Far Away
Stephanie's Ponytail
Munschworks: The First Munsch Collection
Munschworks 2: The Second Munsch Treasury
Munschworks 3: The Third Munsch Treasury
Munschworks 4: The Fourth Munsch Treasury
The Munschworks Grand Treasury
Munsch Mini-Treasury One
Munsch Mini-Treasury Two
Munsch Mini-Treasury Three

For information on these titles please visit www.annickpress.com
Many Munsch titles are available in French and/or Spanish, as well as in
board book and e-book editions. Please contact your favorite supplier.